I0746727

Tina the Tractor

Julia Assatourian

Tina the Tractor

This book is dedicated to Sweet Ellie Holland who loves to hear fun stories

A big Thank You to Eric Joseph my Publishing Manager who gave me lots of support and courage to publish. Also a big 'Thank You' to Emily …. The illustrator who made a wonderful job on bringing Tina the Tractor and friends to life.

Tina was a big, strong red tractor who lived on a big, green farm. She loved her job. Tina liked to feel the sun on her shiny red paint as she rumbled through the fields; she liked the smell of fresh-turned earth and the sound of birds singing.

One sunny morning, Tina was busy pulling a big plough. She was making long, straight lines in the soft soil to plant carrots. A little bunny hopped out of her way, his nose twitching. "Thank you, Tina," he said. "You're making a lovely garden full of carrots for us!"

Tina smiled with her big, metal grille. She likes making the bunnies happy.

Later that day, Tina pulled a big trailer full of hay. Some fluffy sheep were waiting for him. They jumped up and down with joy when they saw the hay. "Thank you, Tina!" they bleated. "You are our best friend".

Tina was happy to help. She likes making the fluffy sheep happy.

As the sun began to set, Tina pulled a big water tank. The cows were waiting for a drink. They mooed happily as they lapped up the cool water. "Thank you, Tina," they said. "You came at the right time! We were thirsty after a day in the field".

Tina was happy to help. She liked making the cows happy.

At the end of the day, Tina was tired but happy. She had helped all the animals on the farm. Tina smiled as she rumbled back to her barn to sleep.